Frog's Summer Journey

Anita Loughrey

Illustrated by Lucy Barnard

Frog sat on a lily pad.
"I've lived here all my life.
It's time I had a change," he thought.

He gazed across the water.
"It's brighter on the other side of
the pond," Frog croaked. "I should
live there. But how can I get across?
It's a long way to swim!"

Fish popped her head out of the water.
"What's wrong, Frog?" she asked.

"I'm going to live on the other side of the pond,
but I don't know how to get there," Frog said.
"I'll nibble through the stem of the lily pad
and you can float across," Fish replied.

Fish gnawed the stem.
The summer sun shone high
in the sky, reflecting on the
surface of the water. Bees buzzed
around the giant water lilies.

Soon the lily pad was free. Frog waved
goodbye to his friend as he floated
to the other side of the pond.

Elegant swans glided past, dipping
their long necks into the water.
A family of ducks paddled over
and dived below the surface.

"This is perfect," thought Frog.

But then...

"That's mine," squawked the swan, tugging at the pondweed. "No, it's mine," quacked the duck, trying to snatch the weed for herself. They pecked and flapped their wings at each other. Feathers flew into the air.

They squabbled
and screeched
and bumped
Frog's lily pad.

Splish!

Splash!

Frog fell into
the water.

Splosh!

"Oh no! I can't live here.
It's far too noisy," Frog croaked.
He scanned the pond for
somewhere else to live.

It looked beautiful and calm
over by the willow, with its long
branches tumbling over the bank.

Frog climbed back onto the lily pad and
paddled away from the squabbling birds,
past dancing dragonflies, until he
reached the willow.

But the willow tree cast a long shadow over the pond. Frog shivered. "Oh no! I can't live here. It's too dark," he thought, "and there are no new lily pads for me to sit on."

"It's brighter over there by the cherry tree," thought Frog, so he crossed the pond again.

A song thrush tweeted above him in the cherry tree, coaxing her chicks out of the nest to fly. "This is lovely. It's not too dark and it's not too noisy."

A cherry splashed into the water, then another, and another. **Plonk!**

Splash!

Plonk!

Frog jumped off the lily pad onto a log just in time. A cherry hit the lily pad, sinking it to the bottom of the pond.

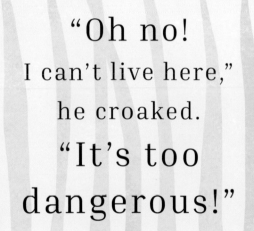

"Oh no!
I can't live here,"
he croaked.
"It's too
dangerous!"

Another large cherry hit
the log, rocking it. Frog
hopped into the reeds.
Crickets chirped loudly.

Frog hopped through the sweet-scented
flowers around the edge of the pond
until he found a sunny spot covered
with bright water lilies.
"This looks like a nice spot," he thought.

Fish popped her head
out of the water.
"Are you back?" she asked.
"Did you find somewhere
nice to live?"

Frog laughed. "You mean I'm home?
I've travelled all around the pond
and found this is the perfect
place to live after all."

Summer Activities

Fun and simple ideas for you and your child to enjoy together.

Paper flower bouquet

1. Cut different colours of tissue paper into squares (the bigger the squares the bigger the flowers).
2. Lay seven squares on top of each other and fold the tissue paper back and forth around the edge, like a fan.
3. Wrap a green pipe cleaner around the middle of the flower underneath and twist it to hold the tissue paper in place.
4. Separate the tissue paper to make the petals.
5. Put four or five flowers together to create a stunning bouquet.

Summer perfume

1. Collect rose petals in a bowl.
2. Add water and leave the rose petals to soak for a few days.
3. Drain away the rose petal pulp and pour the water into a bottle.
4. Dab a little on your wrists.
What does your perfume smell like?

Minibeast hunt

Take a walk in a local park or garden and see what minibeasts live in the different areas. Have a look under rocks, in grass, in trees or under fallen logs. Which minibeasts can you spot? Can you see any bees, crickets or dragonflies? Draw some pictures of the minibeasts you see.

'Signs-of-summer I spy'

Use the pages in this book or go for a summer walk with your child to play 'signs-of-summer I spy'. See what signs of summer you can spot. Say: "I spy with my little eye, a sign of summer beginning with the letter…". For example you could use: 'b' for bee, 'c' for cricket or 'w' for waterlilies.

Did you spot the signs of summer in the story?

White waterlilies were floating on the pond.

In the summer, when the weather is warmer, waterlily flowers are in bloom. They love the sunshine and the still water in ponds. The flowers come in all different colours. They open every morning and close again in the evening. Each flower only lasts about four days.

The Sun was shining high in the sky.

In summer the days are longer. This is because of the tilt of the Earth. The side of the Earth that is tilted closest to the Sun has the longest, brightest days, because it gets more direct light from the Sun's rays.

Sweet-scented summer flowers were in bloom.

There are lots of brightly-coloured flowers that grow in the summer and many of them, like roses and jasmine, have strong scents. The sweet smell and their colour attracts insects to help pollinate the flowers, so they can grow fruit and new seeds.

A song thrush was coaxing her chicks out of their nest to fly.

Young birds will stay close to their parents to be fed, but to survive they need to be able to get food on their own. The parents encourage the young birds to hop on to a branch and test their wings. This helps the young birds learn to look after themselves.

Bees were buzzing around.

There are lots of different kinds of insects buzzing around in summer, including bumblebees and honeybees. Bees are very important as they take the pollen from one flowering plant to another. This helps plants to grow fruit and seeds. Bees have a very good sense of smell, which helps them to recognise the different types of flowers.

FSC
www.fsc.org
MIX
Paper from responsible sources
FSC® C016973

Quarto Knows

Quarto is the authority on a wide range of topics.
Quarto educates, entertains and enriches the lives of our readers—enthusiasts and lovers of hands-on living.
www.quartoknows.com

Editor: Harriet Stone
Designer: Sarah Andrews & Victoria Kimonidou
Author: Anita Loughrey
Illustrator: Lucy Barnard

© 2020 Quarto Publishing plc
This edition first published in 2020 by QED Publishing,
an imprint of The Quarto Group.
The Old Brewery, 6 Blundell Street, London N7 9BH, United Kingdom.
T (0)20 7700 6700 F (0)20 7700 8066
www.QuartoKnows.com

A catalogue record for this book is available from the British Library.

ISBN 978 0 7112 5077 2

Manufactured in Guangdong, China TT122019

9 8 7 6 5 4 3 2 1